The Infidel

The Infidel

Prasanta Patnaik

Translated by
Dr Tapan K Panda

BLACK EAGLE BOOKS
2021

BLACK EAGLE BOOKS

USA address:
7464 Wisdom Lane
Dublin, OH 43016

India address:
E/312, Trident Galaxy, Kalinga Nagar,
Bhubaneswar-751003, Odisha, India

E-mail: info@blackeaglebooks.org
Website: www.blackeaglebooks.org

First International Edition Published by
BLACK EAGLE BOOKS, 2021

THE INFIDEL
by **Prasanta Patnaik**
Translated by **Dr Tapan K Panda**

Original Copyright © **Prasanta Patnaik**
Translation Copyright © **Dr Tapan K Panda**

Cover & Interior Design: Ezy's Publication

ISBN- 978-1-64560-164-7 (Paperback)
Library of Congress Control Number: 2021933806

Printed in United States of America

PREFACE

Sri Prasanta Patnaik, very senior journalist, writer, photo journalist and editor of newspapers in Odisha wrote this novel in 1962 (58 years from now) which was published in 1966. He wrote this novella when he was just 21 year old. However the novella is so relevant that today also the changes that the protagonist hopes to achieve in 1962 is yet to be realized. This book, in true sense is immoral and talks about common man for more than six decades and will continue to do so.

He has written many stories but somewhere I am stuck with this novella for various reasons. Sri Prashant Pattnaik is my childhood buddy Parth Patnaik's father. I had promised uncle sometime back that I would translate the novel to English.

The difficulty of translating this book was twofold: A 50+ guy was translating a 21 year old writer's book after 58 years. The novella is a deadly combination of romance and equitable anguish of a young and independent minded protagonist. The book was published as 'Asati'. I have translated the title as 'Asati-The Adulteress' on the advice of Dr Gopa Nayak. I wish to thank Sri Prashant Patnaik for permitting me to translate and publish the work for a wider audience.

Dr Tapan K Panda
February 15, 2021

1

'Amitav; you are truly bizarre! How many days will you live like this by taking life as a test?'

Lifting the face from the book Amitav looked at Devbandya. She was looking at him with a sense of pride.

Amitav smiled!

The reflection of his laughter was evident on Devbandya's face. He bowed down to focus on his reading. Devbandya moved closed to him and said, "First answer my questions and then you read."

Smilingly Amitav said, "What should I answer to your old question? I can't answer to that question. Only this much can I say that as long as I am alive, I will continue to move towards my goals. Of course; I have to bear pain for this and I will continue to bear in future also. Despite all this, I won't move away from my goals. This is my final decision Devi. I hope you will not ask this question again to me."

Saying this much, he looked at Devbandya to gauze her reaction. Devbandya's eyes were filled with tears. She couldn't utter anything. Amitav smiled by seeing tears in her eyes. He moved close to her and said, "Devi, I am not able to understand why you are so much worried about me. Despite all obstacles in my life, I am accepting them with a smile and will continue to do that. But why are you so much worried about me?"

Wiping out the tears in the corner of the veil Devbandya gazed at Amitav; the same innocent face; there is not an iota of reflection of any annoyance or irritation. She has never seen Amitav being remorse and sitting with a sad face.

Amitav is really very strange. Being so close to him, she is unable to comprehend Amitav. He will remain unresolved forever.

Hiding all the pain within, she said 'You should think about yourself, Amitav!'.

Amitav smiled and said, 'Why, what happened?'

-Your health is on a decline. You may do whatever you wish to, but listen to my request and take care of your health.

-Let it be there Devi. I know you have won many prizes in school in debating on a topic 'health is wealth'. There is no benefit of giving a speech to me because there is nothing more stupid than expecting a prize from me.

Amitav's words must have hurt Devbandya. She hardly uttered a word and looked at Amitav. She couldn't think of anything by which she can convince Amitav.]

Amitav was worried by looking at his wristwatch and said, 'Devi, so much to do. It's already late. I fail to realize how time runs so quickly like a horse whenever I come to you.'

Amitav moved out of the room before Devbandya could utter a word. Devbandya stood near the door and looked at him. Amitav was lost in the street crowd.

Devbandya removed her attention from the crowd and returned to the study room. Like every other day, Amitav stirred a storm inside her. It's rare to have such an indomitable person on earth. Despite that she doesn't know why she loves Amitav so deeply.

Amitav is unique. Devbandya liked every bit of his behaviour - even Amitav's irritation on her.

Wandering on the thoughts of Amitav, her eyes fell on a small packet on the table. She picked up the packet and unwrapped. There was a book, a new book. She lovingly looked at the book. That's Amitav's writing.

The first published book of Amitav! But he didn't by mistake tell her anything about the book!

Devbandya turned the pages. She was overwhelmed in abundant happiness. This was an anthology of all poems in his first published book.

When she saw that the book is dedicated to her, she held the book close to her heart with sheer joy. How much Amitav loves her! Devbandya felt proud on this.

There is definitely some pleasure in loving a strange person like Amitav. Amitav has dedicated the book to her; brought the book for her as a gift but forgot to give the book! He had left the book just as it is on the table. Most often Amitav appears to be absent minded these days. But he has never spoken anything to her about the book. Despite thinking multiple times to ask him, Devbandya couldn't muster courage to question on this. Keeping all her thoughts within, she just gossips around when she is with him.

Once again she opened Amitav's poetry collection. She had a desire to read those poems aloud.

Breaking her thoughts, suddenly Shyamalendu entered inside. Shyamalendu is cousin of Devbandya and a Physics faculty in a local college.

Seeing Shyamalendu, she ran towards him and showing the book she said, "Amitav's book is published. All his poems are included in this and he has dedicated the book to me,'

She said all these in a single breath and then glanced at Shyamalendu. He was serious. That smile when he entered into the room went missing. He said in a serious tone, "Yes, I know. I hope you will never speak to me again about that envelope."

Devbandya felt as if somebody has thrown molten iron on her innocent heart. She never expected to hear such comments about Amitav from Shyamalendu. Devbandya was ready to bear anything except any harsh words against Amitav. So like a wounded tigress, she replied to

Shyamalendu, "How great is Amitav, you don't know Shyamalendu Bhai".

I know; know very well and how big a mistake you have committed by keeping a relationship with Amitav; that is also not unknown to me."

- What do you mean?

- I don't like your friendship with Amitav at all.

- I had an assumption that you are not a petty person. People like you are travelling to moon and mars in rocket speed and I am surprised how you have confined yourself to such a parochial mind!

- I had this feeling that hearts of science students are broader, but how wrong that assumption was -is proved today.

-I can see how you are arguing for Amitav.

- I have learnt from him how to fight for truth and just. Others may not oppose if you say a day as night but I will definitely oppose that.

By listening to Devbandya's words, Shyamalendu felt insulted; agitated and said 'Amitav is characterless"

Hearing Shyamalendu, Devbandya laughed! A laugh filled with reproach! She stopped after a while and said, "Have you seen your image in front of a mirror, brother Shyamalendu?"

Shyamalendu paced towards the veranda before she could say anything else and said, "I am going to put a full stop to your naughtiness. I can watch you being spoiled due to friendship with that rascal."

-I am not spoiled. You, your outlook and mind is spoiled-quite agitated, Devbandya told this.

By that time Shyamalendu had crossed the backyard and gone inside father's drawing room.

Pressing Amitav's book close to the heart, Devbandya returned back to the study room and cried aloud. Words of Shyamalendu started echoing and hurting her even more after he left the room than during his presence. Devbandya lost all her patience and started crying like a helpless child.

2

A mitav returned home around eight in the night. Amitav's rented house was in a dark lane of the town. The distance of Amitav's from Devbandya's house will not be less than three miles. Devbandya's father is a reputed businessman. Devbandya probably would have gone to sleep in her luxurious home. But Amitav had just returned home.

Cycling the old bicycle for the whole day, both the tired legs were not ready to go one step further. Balancing the cycle on the wall, he scouted for the matchbox to light the lamp. Thereafter like every day, he started playing with his favourite dolls. They are friends in the lonely life of Amitav. Whenever alone at home, he plays, talks and laughs aloud with these toys. The old joker on the shelf always had a glimpse of smile on his face. His head starts reeling in slightest of breeze. Amitav went near him and slowly swung his head. He also nodded.

Amitav looked at him and laughed. He remembered about this doll's partner which he had gifted to Devbandya. She has kept it with utmost care in the glass shelf of her study room. This one is lying here among dust in an uncleaned condition. Despite all this, the smile is not receding in the doll's face. As if he is telling him that there is also a pleasure in living like this.

One will be able to understand human values only if one lives like this. One can live on affluence and turn into a lifeless matter or mutate himself to a machine...

Amitav winked; saw the old joker smiling in the same way. Despite his worn out coat, patched pant and bloated tummy, he was smiling and making others to smile...

Amitav started thinking that this toy maker must have been an intelligent person...

Then he started looking at other dolls on the shelf; caressed body of everyone. Leaving apart books, these dolls are friends in his lonely life. At the end of a tired day, when he returns home, the dolls wait for him, as if all of them want to get a touch of his hands. Amitav also forgets his loneliness.

Amitav picked up a book from the shelf and reached to the table. After seeing the letter lying on the table, he realized that he has not returned home from seven in the morning. Postman has gone back throwing the letter through the window.

Tearing the envelope, he started reading the letter. Alphabets are quite known. Younger sister Anita has written the letter.

Brother!

Regards!
It is almost eleven months since you have left the village

and you not returned even once. In between two holidays are over. Everyone staying outside the village came home. You didn't come. Mother felt very sad and sobbed silently. Father said, "He is like this from childhood days. Doesn't matter how much you say, he won't change? He will forget his thirst and hunger if he is preoccupied with work. He must have been thinking about home? But he has always given work as first priority throughout his life. So he must not able to come home due to some work.

Villagers are gossiping a lot. After returning from Katak, Bipin bhai (brother) defamed your name a lot by propagating against you. Despite all these, mother never listens to anyone's words. She always carries the same thought. The holy basil will remain basil even if it is in the burial ground. Tragia involucrata will remain the same even if you keep it in temple. So there is no doubt about you in the family.

Brother, you are writing such good stories and poems but we are not able to read them. Father had brought a magazine where one of your stories was published. Reading that story mother cried with happiness. She has kept the magazine with care on the prayer room's platform. Now onwards, whenever there is a story or poem published in a magazine, please send a copy to me.

Please return to village at least for a day after getting this letter. Maternal grandparents have come to our village. They are anxious to meet you. By the name of nanny, please come for a day. Brother, please do return home for a day."

Yours affectionately
Ani

Reading the letter, pictures of home as well as the village started dancing in front of his eyes; the calm and quite face of younger sister. He started remembering repeatedly about parents, grandparents and other younger sisters. Together all of them started churning Amitav's memory.

Amitav started thinking how truly he had neglected his family. In between two holiday breaks are over but he has not thought in the dream to return to the village. Blindfolded, he is working towards making his dream a success. In between Amitav has turned very selfish!

The truth in each word of Anita's letter started hurting him repeatedly. He writes stories and poems. Others read them. But whether his parents, brothers and sisters read them or not; he has never been careful to know what kind of reactions they have after reading his writings!

Anita has written in the letter that this time, Bipin has spoken ill about him quite a lot in the village. Amitav couldn't understand anything. What can be said to disrepute him? Bipin must have spoken that he is not going to village and has forgotten everyone in the family. But what is Bipin's selfish interest behind this? Amitav remembered about Bipin's father Mr. Hrushikesh Mohanty. He used to get maximum pleasure by talking ill of others. May be Bipin has this ominous characteristic of his father!!

After keeping the letter in the drawer, Amitav tried to sleep but he couldn't. Memories of village, home, parents and brother started hunting him more and more. Anita has written about returning to the village at least for a day.

Maternal grandparents have come. They have not seen Amitav for almost three years. How much happy they will be by seeing him!

Amitav got up and looked at the calendar. Tomorrow is a Sunday. He was mentally assured. He went to sleep after deciding that he would travel to the village tomorrow in the bus.

3

The wall clock rang aloud to sign six o'clock.

Devbandya's mind just fickled. It has been two hours since her return from the college. Amitav is not seen so far? Every day by four thirty, he used to meet Debbandya. Why it is so late today? Devbandya started thinking that in last four years, despite being in Cuttack, there was never been an exceptional day when Amitav had not met her. Has Amitav gone out today? Before leaving, he could have told him or informed someone on phone at home. So what happened to Amitav?

Though woman shows herself to the outside world as strong as possible but her heart within is soft and smooth like rose petals; may get injured in a slightest hit; alone she feels helpless; despite trying as much as possible she cannot suppress weaknesses of her gentle heart. Some kind of a sin touched Debvandya's heart.

Did Amitav meet with an accident? Has he fallen sick? There was no way to get any correct information about him.

Whosoever loves someone deeply, his absence stirs the mind to bring such kind of palpitations. Debbandya started shivering in a similar kind of a stir. But is there a choice? Had Shyamalendu brother not created the storm yesterday, she could have sent a servant to collect information about Amitav. But Shyamalendu brother turned everything upside down. Based on whatever he has told to parents yesterday, though they didn't ask anything, she could see a change in their behaviour. Parents appeared serious. Sister Tuni is also not talking much. But despite putting all efforts and thinking over again and again, she couldn't discover the source of her misatke.

It was seven.

Still Amitav didn't come. Devbandya's eyes were filled with tears. She started thinking that Amitav wouldn't come today. She got up to offer prayer to God. Wherever Amitav is, let him be safe and good.

Hearing this of course, Amitav would have laughed. He was so materialistic and practical! Had he been here now, would have surely said something, "Your god-titled gentleman is definitely a helpful person; who has dedicated himself to do well to others. Starting from making people who don't study well, pass in the examinations and doing all sorts of public welfare activities?"

Amitav has strange arguments!

Had he observed Devbandya's restlessness towards him, he would have said, "Devi! You love me more than myself ... Isn't it? But why so?"

Devbandya couldn't answer to this 'why'. Many a times

she had asked herself why she loves him so much. But never got any answer. There was no selfish interest behind this love. There is no reason… but she loves.

Devbandya couldn't think of anything else. Everything got jumbled up within her brain. Bumping herself onto a pillow and lying on the bed, she cried a lot. She even didn't know why she was crying. May be crying is the only medium to lighten a heavily loaded heart…. inattentively, she had gone to sleep at some time.

4

Amitav was observing everything after reaching the village. He had returned to village after eleven months. But even after these long eleven months, nothing has even marginally changed in the village or at home. Everything is as it was before. He felt as if he had left the village just few days ago.

Sooner did he arrive, the news spread in the village? Amitav had returned to the village after so many days. Mother was quite excited on his arrival. The younger sisters sat around him. Amitav was also gossiping with them.

As soon as he arrived at home, nanny hugged him and said, "Ami! Get married soon. I will go to heaven after cuddling a boy or girl on your lap"

Hearing Nanny's proposition, Amitav didn't utter anything-just smiled. He thought as if elders have no second problem than giving marriage to children or grandchildren.

Filled with happiness and laughs, Amitav's time was moving smoothly in the village. There was no responsibility here, no disturbances, and no tiredness. May be it's for few days but he was enjoying life with amusement and carelessness.

On his return to Cuttack next, there will be again the same routine life. He has to stay in condition of restlessness till results are published. May be he has to find out a specific job after that.

But Amitav's aim in life is different! It is not enough to live by arranging one's bread. It will be a matter of good fortune to arrange food for hundreds of hungry people.

Amitav was on a day dream. When will he succeed on his goals? He will publish a weekly newspaper through which he will announce a war against corruption, hunger and illiteracy. Development of a nation is not possible as long as there exist two communities of 'the exploiters' and 'the exploited'. So he has to wage a war to uproot the corrupt exploiter community from the society. Doesn't matter how difficult it is, he won't deviate from this goal. This is his life's mission. But for this- he needs funds. Amitav is penniless. Post appearing his master's examination, whatever he earned from a job in a newspaper is not enough to cover his personal expenses.

Editing a magazine is like a flower from the sky. But efforts are necessary to catch that sky flower. Commitment is required. Amitav has impregnable trust on his energy levels to achieve this dream. He was preoccupied with such a strange passion. He couldn't have returned home due to this preoccupation.

Bishnuprashad came home exactly at seven in the evening. He was Amitav's childhood friend who dropped from college to start a business. But he had not forgotten his close friendship with Amitav. That's why he came to meet him on hearing about his arrival. In between Bishnuprashad's health had improved- with a bulging tummy and receding hairline. A bald head is a symbol of rich people.

Seeing Bishnuprashad, happily Amitav embraced him. They are meeting after long eleven months. Two friends started chatting with each other.

They gossiped a lot. In between the conversation, by pressing Amitav's hand, Bishnuprasad said, "Brother, I will ask you a question- please tell me the truth?".

-Have I ever lied to you? Amitav responded with a smile.

With reluctance, Bishnuprashad asked "You won't mind?"

-No- please tell me.

-There is a big campaign here!

-What's the matter?
...
-Why don't you tell me? Am I going to behead you or what?

-I heard you are getting married somewhere in Cuttack.

Amitav with a smile asked "to whom?"

"Some big businessman's daughter-that's the reason for which you were not coming to the village. Brother- you will be in a ditch if you trust these urban girls! They will transform a young guy into a sheep!"

Amitav felt the pain of a lightning after hearing Bishnuprashad. He became a bit serious and asked. "Who has given this useless news- let me know."

"Array- have we gone to Cuttack or known anyone? On his return from the town, Bipin has spread this rumour in the whole village. The girl is studying in a college; very fair complexioned and beautiful; being greedy for her wealth, you are marrying there!"

Amitav couldn't think of what to answer. Staying silent for few moments, he said, "You know me from childhood days. There is no point in giving an explanation on this matter. Just wait. Truth is always eternal. So automatically you will know."

Don't know what Bishnuprashad understood from these words, he didn't utter anything on this topic and started gossiping on other topics.

After Bishnuprasad's return and post dinner, he went to bed but couldn't catch sleep. He started thinking how Bipin has polluted the village environment by spreading the news linking him with Devbandya.

Devbandya! That simple, calm girl had taken a place in his mind. Devbandya is an exception in the modern and rich society. She is the daughter of a businessman who belongs to a capitalist group that multiplies their wealth hundred times by sucking blood and exploiting the hard working labour class proletariats. Despite all this, Amitav loves her. He didn't have the power to refuse her simplicity, show lesser thoughts and express pure love. That's why he had conceded defeat in front of Devbandya.

For the first time he felt that his relationship with Devbandya can also be seen with suspicion. He recalled about Anita's letter. She had given a hint in her letter on what Bipin had spoken about.

Amitav smiled! Really how strange these people are!

5

Devbandya was gazing through the open window.

Amitav had come few moments before. He informed that he suddenly left for the home yesterday. Hearing this, Devbandya felt very happy. Prior to this, many a times, she had requested Amitav to make a round trip to the village during holidays. But Amitav had earlier ignored her words with a smile.

Amitav is really bizarre! He works relentlessly over day and night. Despite that she has never seen an iota of sadness in him. Man has to do everything. Unless you work on, nobody will do it for you. He is of the opinion that relying on God and without putting any effort is the greatest stupidity. That's the reason why he remains always preoccupied. He has a firm belief on his power and capabilities. May God bless Amitav!

Devbandya wondered why she was thinking so much about Amitav. Why she gets worried about him. Why she becomes impatient if she doesn't see him for a day. Amitav is nobody for her. She even doesn't have this much of restlessness within her for own family members.

All these questions of Devbandya spontaneously melt within herself. She can't think anything beyond. She sat with closed eyes. Thoughts of Amitav keep on roaming in her mind- like a naughty and impenetrable child. Probably Devbandya enjoys most while thinking about Amitav.

Amitav told her that he is going to Kolkata same night. He will return approximately after a week or so. He is going on some urgent work of the newspaper office in which he is employed. He may not be able to meet Devbandya before leaving for Kolkata. All these seven days will emerge like a lot of many more days. What is the choice then?

Devbandya was observing drastic changes in her house in last two days. Shyamalendu bhai had come once again last night. For quite a long time, he had some closed door meetings with parents and Sister Tuni. Today morning father has called up brother Abhay via a trunk call. Father was talking about some urgent work. What kind of urgent work might be there? Devbandya had a wish to ask father. But she couldn't dare. She couldn't ask anyone in the house also. Everyone is behaving odd by keeping some distance from her. Whom she could have asked?

Brother Abhay is a gentleman. No other husband will have as much love as he has for sister Tuni. Brother Abhay also loves Devbandya nonetheless. Devbandya hardly takes special care about herself or her clothes. He calls her as 'mental' for her poor dress sense despite being daughter of a richman.

Devbandya likes brother Abhay's address to her as a mental-as if all the care and closeness are embedded in that address.

Abhay never behaves with her like any other brother in laws.

Brother Abhay is a deputy magistrate. Now he lives in Puri. Father must have told him many times, "Abhay, quit your job and look after my business. Whatever you are getting from your job is not enough for your expenses. What will you do for your children?"

Brother Abhay remains silent. He may not like to stay with father.

She will definitely ask brother Abhay tonight about this urgent work for which father has called him. Even if she can't ask anyone else but definitely she can ask him.

6

Devbandya was feeling sick in that evening- that's why she went to bed a bit early. Waking up from the bed in the morning she heard that Abhay has reached around 9 PM last night. She went to meet Abhay. He was having tea at that time. She did 'namaskaar' to him. Abhay gave a remorse look to her. Then he appeared serious. He didn't call her as 'mental' like all other days. Devbandya felt hurt due to change in his behavior. Her eyes become teary.

Other than responding to her 'namaskar' brother Abhay didn't utter a single word to her. He started chatting with sister Tuni – as if he was deliberately neglecting Devbandya's presence.

Mini came during this time. Mini is Devbandya's younger sister. This year she has registered for her college after completing matric. Mini is very careless.

Moving closer to Abhay , Mini asked, " Oh! Sahib! Are you leaving today?"

With a smile, Abhay pulled her arms and said, "Yes, will you not come with me?"

While freeing her arms from his clutches, Mini naughtily responded, "Why should I go when sister Tuni is there?"

The she almost ran away from there.

Devbandya was observing all these like a lifeless statue. She doesn't know how to joke also. Many get annoyed with her for this. She can't gossip just like that. Some people misinterpret this as her high society arrogance. Despite all this, she can bear them. But Mini is an expert on all these matters. She can gossip with others for hours. She can be a lot playful.

Brother Abhay gave a look to Devbandya and turned away. Devbandya couldn't further stand there with patience. She ran back and straight fell over on the bed. Despite thinking a lot she couldn't resolve why people are behaving this way with her. She has not harmed anyone.

Blocking her thoughts, Mini suddenly entered inside. Lying down next to Devbandya, she started laughing aloud.

Devbandya looked up and asked, "What happened; Mina?"

Nothing

Then why are you laughing like this?

There is a funny thing!

What?

No, I won't tell you.

Why? Will it be a crime if I know about this?

No, it's not like that. What will you give me if I tell you all this? I will share big news!

No! I cannot bribe to get only news!

All your ideology will be dismantled after few days.

Why so?

You will automatically come to know. You will end up crying by serving your husband and in-laws. When will you show your ideology?

Why are you talking rubbish?

That's why I was refusing to delve? Am I saying all this on my own? There was a conversation about your marriage till 2 AM last night. Your marriage is going to happen in next ten to fifteen days.

How did you know about this?

I was listening to all this on the other side of the window.

Who was talking about this?

Last night brother Shyamalendu had come. There was a joint discussion on this topic involving father, mother, brother Abhay, sister Tuni and brother Shyamalendu.

Hearing all this, Devbandya's face turned pale. She was

unaware of the fact that, in between such a conspiracy had been hatched against her.

Before she could think anything else- she remembered Amitav. One day in an evening, he had asked to Devbandya, "Devi, now you get worried even if I come late for a day; what will happen after your marriage?"

She didn't give any answer on that day. There was no need to give an answer then. But today she has to find out the answer to that old question. She will never be able to get a chance to meet or talk to Amitav on daily basis if she gets married in between. Then what shall she do? Devbandya felt an impossible flare within. That fire started growing within. The waves of questions deep inside her started rising up like sea surf and then continued melting down.

7

Amitav returned from Kolkata after ten days. Upon arrival in Cuttack, he immediately rushed to Devbandya's house. By that time Devbandya was looking through the open window. She was so absent minded that she couldn't realize Amitav's presence. Moving nearer to her he asked, "Why are you looking so remorse?"

Returning to senses after hearing the question, Devi looked at him. But she couldn't utter a single word. She felt as if her throat is getting chocked. She couldn't conclude what to speak to Amitav after seeing him after such a long gap.

She only glanced at him.

With a smile, Amitav said, "Devi, you are looking at me as if I am an unknown person?"

Devbandya was dumbstruck.

She was thinking about Amitav. How deeply she loves him. How special is Amitav compared to others! She had a desire to open up to Amitav and tell him how a conspiracy was hatched against her in the family. Her marriage is due in two days. What kind of reaction Amitav will have after hearing the news of her sudden marriage. And if he asks about the reasons for which her parents have taken such a decision? Then what answer will she give?

You are silent Devi?

Amitav again asked her.

Devbandya's eyes were filled with tears.

Devi! you are crying?

Impatiently Amitav asked. Tears in her eyes today appeared surprisingly new to Amitav who had seen tears in her eyes many a times over last four year long relationship. Devbandya is very emotional. She starts crying on small matters. Sometimes Amitav calls her as a crybaby. But Amitav lost his patience by seeing tears in her eyes today. Anxiously he asked, "What has happened to you?"

Despite this, Devbandya was at a loss of words. What answer will she give- What will she say about what has happened to her?

Amitav became serious and said, "Are you angry on me? It's OK. I am leaving now. I will never come back to irritate you".

Amitav got ready to leave the place.

Devbandya had a desire to hug him hard and cry a lot. She couldn't bear it anymore. She started crying aloud.

Amitav was surprised seeing her crying. As if the tears were flowing by injuring the inner core of her heart. He couldn't comprehend anything. Returning back, he stood near her and said, "Hey! Devi- you are a crying baby- crying like a little baby- anyone who sees this will surely laugh."

The uncontrolled tears started flowing on Devbandya's face like wild spring.

Amitav was looking at her face like an innocent child. But he couldn't decide what to speak to console her. He was feeling like a culprit -as if he was responsible for such intense crying of Devbandya.

Controlling her sigh after a while, she said- Do you know Amitav?

What? Amitav asked with a worry.

In between father has taken an ultimate decision.

Let me hear what is that decision?

Mine and Meena's marriage is scheduled after two days!

Amitav got joyful after hearing this. He laughed and said, "Wah! It's a wonderful decision. Why to cry on this matter? Devi- with whom your and Mina's marriages are being settled?"

Devbandya looked at the wonderful animal named Amitav with astonishment.

How strange is this Amitav? She had a guess that, Amitav would feel sad after hearing the news of her marriage. But Amitav's face glowed up after hearing this news. Being speechless, she continued to look at his face.

Without getting an answer from Devbandya, Amitav anxiously asked, "Why are you silent Devi? Are you feeling ashamed to tell me?"

In a serious tone, Devbandya replied- My marriage is fixed with engineer Bikram Mohanty and Mina will marry Dr. Sitakanta Das.

Hearing the name of Bikram Mohanty, jolly well Amitav started dancing. He said with a laugh, "Devi! Do you know who Bikram Mohanty is? He is my childhood friend. Now he lives with all the comfort. In few days of joining the job, he has built a house and owns a car also.

'Who is living with all happiness- Amitav?' Listening to the question in a heavy accent, Amitav looked back to see Sharada Prasanna Chaudhari entering into the room.

Devbandya shivered in an unknown consternation!

Amitav said with a laugh, "I was talking about Bikram. He is my childhood day friend and a very good guy."

Before Amitav could utter anything else, Sharada Prasanna roared back- Shut up Amitav! I don't need to get a certificate about my would-be son-in-law from a characterless person like you."

Amitav said in an unshaken voice, "You must be misunderstanding me. I was not giving a certificate to Bikram."

-Don't talk that nonsense. I am aware - though you are poor, but you put high values for status, respect and prestige. Devbandya and Minati's marriage is left with two more days. I am hopeful that keeping your self-respect and prestige in mind, you will not try unsuccessfully to stand in front of my door. You can easily comprehend what will be the consequence if you attempt to blur my status and prestige.

Unfettered by the statements of Sharada Prasanna, smilingly Amitav said- I am thankful to you for the advice. But before I leave this place; there will be a day when you will realize that it's not my profession to tarnish image and prestige of someone in the society –that may be your profession!

Without waiting for a word either from Sharada Prasanna or Devbandya; Amitav paced himself out of the room.

Devbandya started crying. Sharada Prasanna took her into arms and said- My child! You are crying! What could have happened if the shadows of that characterless person would have fallen on this auspicious day! If you start giving value to these fallen and poor guys, they may end up harming some or other way. That's why you should shut them up.

Devbandya couldn't say anything further. She was deeply hurt due to her father's allegations against Amitav. Unable to control her sadness, she started crying aloud.

8

Sharada Prasanna's house was jam packed with guests. Today is marriage of Devbandya and Minati. Sharada Prasanna's aristocratic home was decorated with multiple colors of light. The band party was playing the tunes of some popular movie songs. The clarinet was lamenting in between. The waves of happiness were evident on everybody's face. Devbandya and Minati were sitting with a complete makeup. Nobody called Mini as Madhuchhanda. But everybody was acquainted with her name as Madhuchhanda in both school register and marriage invitation card. An environment of bliss and happiness was prevailing everywhere. All around was lighted with neon lamps and decorated with colorful lights.

Amidst all these sources of lights, suppressing her darkness within, Devbandya was crying. She was experiencing darkness all around. Her father's words about Amitav were echoing in her ears- Amitav is profligate. No... that can't happen. Amitav is God. One cannot blur his name. Despite so much of insult inflicted upon him by father, he left the place with a smile. Father said Amitav is an unholy planet! How can a father utter such a mean thing? Amitav may be poor but he is conscious about his self- respect. He who knows how to respect others deserves it. But father had insulted him. He has to suffer the consequences.

Amitav left on that day. He didn't return after that. Why should he have returned? Devbandya couldn't keep track of any news related to him. What happened to Amitav? If he would have done something due to that insult!

No... No... that can't happen! Amitav is not a person with low patience. He has lots of confidence and trust on himself and Devi. Let Amitav live happily. Let his dreams fructify. Devbandya paid respect to God. May God keep Amitav happy? Let God help him on his pathway of life.

The clarinet was crying outside. It's too much of crowd and deafening band party music. The sum of the noise was creating an awful sound. Devbandya had a wish to run away from these lights and from this human forest to a lonely place nearer to Amitav and cry a lot-and to say sorry for father's misconduct. If she could get an opportunity to meet Amitav at least once before the marriage, she could open the endless pain within her and asked for his blessing for her cozy life. Amitav is kind hearted. He will surely bless her. With a smile he would definitely say- "Devi; let the path be filled with flowers with your new friend".

But Amitav was not there today. He is away and far away from her. He may be busy playing with the dolls in his rented house in some lonely lane or planning his future course of action. He knows today is his intimate Devi's marriage day. He will definitely bless him from there.

Observing Devbandya silently thinking about something,

Arupa asked, "What are you thinking now? Are you now thinking about how you are going to address your engineer husband in the first meeting?".

Arupa is a friend of Devbandya. Being a very intimate friend, it is a hobby to tease her with such naughty conversations.

Hearing her question, Devi smiled a bit. She has not thought anything about her future. Now she will run her family with engineer Bikram Mohanty. She should think a bit about him. Amitav is past.

Amitav was also saying the same thing one day- "Devi! I doubt whether we can meet again after your marriage. I will be your past. It will be foolish on your part to think about me. You will be always preoccupied with the future of your husband and children. If I ever return back to your memory, knowingly evict me out like a bad dream. If you always keep on thinking about the past, you may fall back in this materialistic world. You have to run in a future direction. You may lose if you continue to look back."

On that day, Devi had told him-"Amitav, you will always remain within me as that strange, special, atheist and workaholic Amitav. I will never be able to move an inch if I forget you and your ideology. It is possible to build the future on the foundation of the past. There is no meaning of future eliciting the past. This is an impossible proposition like building a castle in the sky."

Amitav had laughed a lot on that day. He had told- "Now I am accepting my defeat in front of your strange arguments.

But you should always remember the far fetching distance between imagination and reality. Then you will lose in front of your own arguments."

Devbandya started imagining whether Amitav's words will emerge as truth. Will she forget Amitav after her marriage?

Engineer Bikram Mohanty suddenly entered into her thoughts. She neither knows him nor seen him. She has only seen his photograph. Mini had stolen the photo from mother's almirah on that night. He was very handsome, healthy; the aristocracy was evident from his appearance and attire. She has to settle down with an unknown person to run her family. He will be everything to her.

What about Amitav?

What will happen to her fate if Bikram also misunderstands her relationship with Amitav like many others? Not everybody's heart is as broad as Amitav. What answer will she give if he ever asks few questions about the relationship with Amitav? And if he misunderstands her then she will be doomed. Devbandya shivered with an unknown pain. She could not think further. Few drops of tear rolled down her white cheeks.

Again being naughty, Arupa asked- "What Devi? Is he a lion or a bear that you are crying being so scared? Brother is a good man; he is an engineer, he must have planned many Taj Mahals for you. His dreams will be meaningful on your arrival. And you are crying!"

Devbandya couldn't control herself any more. Embracing

Arupa, she started sobbing. Encircling her, other friends of Devbandya started joking and teasing her. But nothing entered into her deafened ears. She was crying like a helpless fawn.

A bit away, Mina – Madhuchhanda without an iota of sadness and grief; with complete makeup, was sitting with her friends. She was chatting with friends with ease. By seeing Devbandya's cry, she came closer and said- "Sister, why are you so nervous? Brother Amitav had said in the past – in any given situation; doesn't matter how adverse it may be, if you face it with a smile then you will surely be the winner."

Devbandya started shrieking cry. She doesn't want a win. She wants to remain defeated as she always remained so with Amitav. She was always eager to get each drop of his care and good wishes. In the same way, she wants to remain defeated against engineer Bikram Mohanty. But Bikram will be her husband.

But Amitav- what is he to her? He is nothing but everything to her.

Suddenly the house became noisy. Everyone turned active. There was only one word with everyone- the groom is coming. So everyone became attentive to welcome them. Devbandya was sitting with heads down. Holding onto the immense darkness within her- she was crying profusely.

9

Amidst the hobble bubble, there prevailed a sudden and impossible level of silence and lifelessness-everybody was dumb founded and immobile. Sharada Prasanna was siting like a defeated soldier. The groom is coming; have toured the city with procession and fanfare. The entourage will reach his home in half an hour. But Sharada Prasanna was there without uttering a single word. Devbandya's mother, Sister Tuni, brother Abhaya – every one of them were sitting wordless. Few minutes before, father of Bikram-would be son –in-law of Sharada Prasanna has sent a hand written letter. After reading the letter, Sharada Prasanna handed over the letter to Abhay. Abhay read the content of the letter to Tuni apa, mother and others. Following was written in the letter

Dear Sharada Prasanna Babu
My regards to you; without verifying the correct news about your daughter, I had travelled quite a distance with you in the process of making Devbandya as our daughter- in- law. But it is a matter of regret that Bikram told me straight that he is not going to marry Devbandya. He is of the opinion that she is characterless. She had an illicit relationship with Amitav- the recently published poetry book is a clear proof of this. He has dedicated the book to Devbandya. You are aware about the tradition and status of my clan. Knowingly

I cannot accept Devbandya as my daughter in law. Hope you will not misunderstand me.

Yours sincerely
Chakra Dhar Mohanty

The thunderbolt fell on everybody's head. Mother started lamenting with a cry. Sharada Prasanna roared like a wounded lion- "Knowingly Amitav has destroyed me. I will shoot to kill that rascal."

Sister Tuni straight went to Devbandya and handed over the letter to her. Reading the letter, Devbandya gazed the floor silently. Sister Tuni initiated the conversation- 'You are not a human being Devi. You are a stone- you are a scandal for our family- Do you know what is going to happen? A girl like you should make a suicide."

Devi was there like a stone. Truly she was no more human-she was a statue of stone – for last few days she had turned into a stone. He heart was softer than flowers. But the same is stronger than a rock now. Sister Tuni is saying that she should kill herself. Devbandya laughed by herself- nobody can steal her right to live. She will live. She will love for truth- for Amitav. She will live to prove stainless image of Amitav in front of others.

Sister Tuni continued her limitless abuse. Devbandya was not playing slightest of attention to the same. Everybody was accusing her to be characterless. She has lost her path, she is infidel- whose proof is the piece of Amitav's gifted book. She smiled within again. Amitav is not a human being, he is God and all those people who are trying to accuse him will lose some or other day. Truth's existence has not yet been wiped out from earth's face. Will not all realize the truth of the relationship with Devi someday?

Unfettered, sister Tuni continued abusing her. Circumspecting around her, each one of them were gazing with a sense of abetment. Sister Tuni continued- "If one can find that beggar, characterless Amitav in front- should shoot him like a dog. Someone devoid of any social standing tried to scandalize the other person's pride and status."

As if suddenly Devbandya had fire on her blood. She had head reeling. She was willing to bear all the false accusations, abuses against her- but not ready to hear a single word against Amitav. She had a desire that despite all this- she should open her mouth to warn Sister Tuni. But she remained silent. Her heart was filled with hatred against family members and society.

Sister Tuni moved closer to her and said- "Oh! Bad Omen- laden with all these jewels and gold; Are you not ashamed of sitting here and shading your crocodile tears?"

Devbandya couldn't control her patience- she yelled. Like before; sister Tuni continued her abuses. Seeing such a miserable condition of Devbandya, even Arupa couldn't hold on to her patience level; took her into her lap and started sobbing.

Someone gave news that younger son-in-law has arrived closer to home. Then only, suddenly everyone got up like a sleeping volcano. Everybody started worrying about welcoming and treating the groom; his entourage and further arrangements on the marriage.

Devbandya was still sitting there like a stone statue. Despite so much light around her, she was not able to trace her path within the deep darkness. Many a thoughts started swirling in her mind.

By neglecting Devbandya, on the same way as people give a hatred look at left-overs and useless items in the municipality dustbin, everybody stayed busy on the arrangements for Madhuchhanda marriage.

10

Marriage got solemnized. Madhuchhanda left with her husband. She wanted to speak and meet Devbandya before leaving; but everyone refused her to do so. Sara aunty said, "she is a bad omen, there will be no welfare to you if you see her.'

Madhuchhanda cried.

Devbandya also cried.

Everyone's eyes were filled with tears seeing Madhuchhanda cry. But nobody paid any attention to Devbandya. Madhuchhanda is leaving home to a new place. She will manage her household chore with peace and happiness and will return home as a guest only. What about Devbandya? Will she remain ever as a black spot on clan's reputation?

Madhuchhanda had bid farewell for a while now. Her husband is a doctor. Madhuchhanda should live with all happiness. A careless and innocent girl like her should live happily ever after in life. Let her life be filled with bliss.

And Devbandya! She will probably blaze like this whole of her life. There is none to rescue her from the pain of embezzlement. Amitav is insulted. She couldn't track any news about her. Will Amitav ever meet his so intimate and favorite Devi despite so much of insult? Will it be possible?

Devbandya was crying. The spring of tear from her eyes has dried down for a very long time. She continued sitting there like a lifeless statue. What would have been the reaction of Amitav in this situation, had he been around her? Has he received the pathetic news about Devbandya?

Amitav was saying that engineer Bikram is his childhood day friend... no... that can never be true! Amitav is not a human being... he is God. But Bikram Mohanty- who misunderstood the relationship of Amitav with Devbandya can be so petty! He is like an insect in the hell. He doesn't deserve to be Amitav's friend.

While scolding her, sister Tuni and Sara aunty were saying, "That scoundrel; idiot has spoiled reputation of our family. This alanic was not sipping water without taking his name- Amitav. She was saying that he is God. Showing affection, that sash wrote a poetry book to gift her. This poor girl used to walk with so much of arrogance and used to say – Amitav loves me more than his own younger sister. Now she has to repent for her whole life. What will that scoundrel lose?"

Devbandya's ears stopped responding to all this. The society says she is an infidel. The poetry book gifted by Amitav is the proof of the same. The society could award her so easily the title of a characterless and beige. Will she accept this unwelcome title so easily? No.....she will revolt. She wants to go through the test of fire. If she is burnt alive and turned into ashes in that test, then her name will be lost forever but the obloquy of being characterless and infidel will remain forever. No… that can't happen. Bowing down her head, Devbandya cannot accept this scandal silently. Amitav's own Devi cannot be so petty? She wants Amitav's name not to be tarnished. Amitav is great….

But Devbandya was helpless today. Who else was there to console her for the pain? Amitav is also away from her. Knowingly Amitav has been distanced from her by a conspiracy. So what can she do?

Devbandya was experiencing chuck bumble. Will she remain as a lonely bird forever?

11

Sharada Prasanna was getting worried. He was thinking that Devbandya would remain forever a stigma for him.

It is almost a month now. Sharada Prasanna had failed miserably on all his attempts to find a groom for Devbandya. Wherever he sends a proposal, people start asking many questions. Someone is asking why the elder one is still unmarried after the youngest one being out of home after marriage. Others are saying that they know everything about his daughter. This matter is being the talk of the street and how knowingly they will accept a girl like this....

So Devbandya will always remain as a spinster for whole of her life?

Sharada Prasanna could not think further. Despite being such a powerful and successful businessman, he was unable to find a groom for his daughter.

Shyamalendu is also not seen for many a days. With what a face he will come and meet Sharada Prasanna? Bikram has made a registry marriage with his sister Shyamali. Both of them have left home. Shyamalendu has arranged Bikram's marriage with Devbandya. But nobody knows whereabouts of Bikram and Shyamali. Being in love with Shyamali, Bikram probably have made such an excuse to not marry Devbandya. What can be done in the current situation? Nobody can bring back the wellspring of time.

Shyamalendu's younger brother, Hemkanta said that whatever was to happen has already happened. It will be prudent in current situation to solemnize marriage of Devbandya with Amitav.

Hearing Hemkanta, Sharada Prasanna got angry and said – This can never happen. Devbandya may remain as a spinster throughout her life but he won't solemnize marriage of his daughter with a characterless beggar like Amitav.

Hemkanta remained silent after this.

Abhay said, "I knew this before that Devbandya would have a fate like this. Amitav appears like a first grade scoundrel. The rascal has spoiled her life forever!"

Hemkanta replied, "No brother, you are misreading Amitav". I know him very well but...

Before he could say anything else, Abhay said in an agitated tone, "The kind of person you are, you will only lobby for similar kind of people? Do you now Amitav drinks?"

-How do you know this?

- Shyamalendu was talking about this.

-What did he say?

-He was saying that the house in which Amitav lives is unhygienic and full of wine bottles.

- You must be having a nightmare about Amitav. I won't say anything beyond this. I can affirmatively say that brother Shyamalendu has not seen his residence at all. Whatever un-embellished residence you are talking about, the house is not that bad. Rather you can call the same as a place of pilgrimage. What can be said if you call a house filled with numerous books, magazines and dolls as hell....

-You may stop your speech Hemkanta. What more unfortunate it can be other than discussing about an dirty individual like Amitav.

After this conversation, Hemkanta remained silent and left the place.

12

Devbandya remained as an eyesore to people both inside and outside the house. She couldn't decide what to or not to do. Despite everybody cursing her, mother couldn't say a word to her. But silently she was crying a lot. Often holding her in the lap, she was lamenting about her future. Devbandya also cried. But this flow of tears was incapable of washing anyone's suffering.

It's almost eight o'clock in the night. The moon was like bread (roti) in the sky. All alone on the roof top, Devbandya was gazing at the sky. She was suddenly shocked to hear sound of someone's footsteps. Brother Hemkanta was carefully moving towards her in silence. Devbandya was astonished. She experienced as if her heart has seized to beat. She had a desire to run away from there or start shouting.

Why is this expedition for brother Hemkanta? Feeling as if she has lost all her power, she suddenly opened her mouth to shout at. Brother Hemkanta, by that time, had moved closer to her. He put his right palm on her mouth before she could shout and said- "Don't get scared. I have not come here to harm you like brother Shyamalendu. I have come here to give a piece of news."

Devbandya looked at him in bewilderment. Just moving a

bit away from her, he said- "Though I have come to your home from evening five, but was not finding it convenient to meet you. That's why I have come now to talk to you in tranquility.

Devbandya could compose herself a bit and said- "what is the news brother Hemkanta?"

After resigning, Amitav has left his job. I have visited his home after getting this news. But he was not at home. I couldn't understand the circumstances.

Devbandya couldn't say anything. What can she say? After remaining silent for a while, she said- brother Hema; please go away from this place. Please leave me alone. If you utter Amitav's name in an unholy place like my home, his pious name will be stigmatized.

'You are speaking the truth Devbandya, I am leaving now'- Hemkanta left the place.

Devbandya continued to be there looking at the lonely and desolate sky. She felt as if there was a burden on her shoulders. The load of a corpse- The corpse is of her past; of her personality- that personality which has been knowingly strangulated.

Devbandya looked up the sky. The moon was smiling. Everywhere was flooded with white moon beam - but the darkness of ages had descended within her.

Amitav had left the job? What will he do? He may not stay here. He may go elsewhere leaving this big city. But will

Amitav do that? Can she stay away leaving Cuttack city? Many a times, Amitav has said that the water, air, pebbles and sand of the city is so dear to him that it seems impossible for him to think about leaving the city.

Devbandya recalled about one similar moonlit night. She was roaming on the roof top with Amitav- Looking at the moon, he asked her- Devi- This moon is an ugly thing- isn't it?

Astonishingly Devbandya has questioned - why?

Amitav smilingly said- See, the moon is only enlightening from outside- but what about the light within all of us?

With a laugh, Devbandya has said on that day- Your thoughts are weird!

Amitav also laughed. His set of teeth was signing in the moonlight.

Amitav is really strange. Everything about him is weird. His thoughts are also odd. He must have left the job for some weird reasons. But for once he is not going to meet Devbandya!

Devbandya started shivering once this question came into her mind. No, that shouldn't happen. At least she should meet Amitav before her death. And on that meeting moment falling on his feet, she will beg excuse for the atrocities against him by her father and other family members. She has no more wish. She just had the last desire to meet Amitav for once.

13

Hearing sound of someone's knocking on the door; Amitav paused from writing and looked at his watch. It was half past one in the night.

Who was knocking so late in the night? He left the pen on the table and as soon as he opened the door, Bikram Mohanty entered into the room in a drunken condition. He could smell the ardent smell of alcohol. Amitav couldn't believe to his eyes.

Bikram sat on Amitav's bed in an inebriated condition. Amitav went near him and touching his shoulders, asked him- "Bikram, at so late in night, in such a condition?"

Bikram guffawed. In that dreaded night, the words of his howl reverberated on the room walls and returned back as a deformed noise.

Bikram became serious and after a while glanced at Amitav and said- You must not have expected to see me in this condition Amitav. But not once, many a times in last few days I am drunk like this, alcohol is the only instrument to forget all my sorrows.

But what's your sorrow Bikram? You are leading a good life.

He laughed again and then said- Amitav, what is your opinion about women?

-What do you mean?

Amitav gave a surprised look to Bikram.

-Means- your personal opinion about women- in general?

-But why are you asking this odd question?

-This is not an odd question. This world is strange, do you know the meaning of the word 'ladies'? Ladies are hell! They are fire. The attractive power of this fire is higher than the gravitational power of the earth. That attraction pulls us in so much sometimes that….

- Dropping your philosophical ideologues, I am telling you to sleep silently. I know you are not talking all this- the alcohol as a figurine within you is saying all these things.

-I have not come here to sleep Amitav. We are meeting after so many days and I have come to chat with you. If I won't speak about my sorrows to you, whom else will I speak to?

-Let me hear what is your sorrow?

-Shyamali!

-Meaning?

-Being in love with Shyamali, I was the one who spread grapevine to tarnish her character; projecting her as an adulteress and not letting Devbandya marry anyone. I was the one who told everyone that you had an illicit relationship with her. I left for home and did a registry marriage with Shyamali. But you know- Shyamali is not a woman- she is hell! She is a boiling pot in an ever-gasping flame of a torch. Her wish is to turn me into ashes and embrace someone else…. And I am drinking to recluse myself from that hell.

-But can you save yourself from that hell by drinking? Cowards and impotent drink alcohol; drinking is a hobby for escapists- drinking is nothing but temporary suicide.

- You are right Amitav. I am a coward and a nut because I am killing myself in a momentary grief and yet returning to life next moment! But I don't wish to die like this… I will live… I am drinking to free myself from the fire of these memories.

- will you be able to forget your past just by drinking?

- Umm

-Amitav

- I know there is nothing that can heal the wound in a heart.

-Amitav

- Oh! Bikram, you are crying? –Surprised by seeing tears in Bikram's eyes, Amitav questioned.

Without uttering a single word, Bikram got up, gave a tight hug to Amitav and started wailing.

14

Amitav had a meeting with Hemakant. He was a colleague and shared a cordial relationship with Amitav. He was meeting with Amitav to talk about Devbandya. After listening to everything that Hemkanta had to say, Amitav remained silent as if he has not heard anything. What kind of help he can give to Devi in the emergent situation?

Hemkanta enquired about all the gossip mongering inside the office. The newspaper owner- a friend to Sharada Prasanna; based on a tip from him has already decided to terminate Amitav from the job. Once Amitav heard this grapevine, without giving a chance to remove, he resigned himself from the job.

Without any reaction, Amitav said – I am trying to launch a weekly magazine independently from coming fifteenth August. I have left my job for this reason.

Amitav's dream ought to fructify. He will publish a weekly magazine on his own effort. Amitav couldn't be completely happy within. He felt as if something was missing in his life. Sooner he was moving closer to fulfilling his ultimate wish. But deep within himself he was not happy. He had a sense as if he was deprived of something; as if he has committed a heinous crime- as if he is responsible for Devbandya's misfortune by dedicating the book to her. Else she would have been happier; settled in life and being busy with household chore.

Poor soul would not have faced such a misfortune. But what can Amitav do now?

Amitav felt as if he has turned selfish. He is only bothered about his selfish interest- desperate to fulfill his dream. He had not prepared anything to rebuild Devi's fractured life. He started to think about her- felt sad- turned sentimental.

But has he done anything meaningful for her? What else he could have done? He was banished from touching the footsteps of Sharada Prasanna's house. If he does anything now for Devi's welfare, the same may return as a bad omen to her. So he felt being incapable of doing anything else other than thinking and feeling sorry for her.

Very often his mind turns rebellious. He feels like killing these torch bearers of the society in the middle of the road like the way it was done to Czars in Russia. How much fallen, treacherous and mean minded these people can be! They see the world through a blue glass. It is natural that everything will seem blue. But for how many days are all these? For how long one can bear the tyranny of these monarchs? Misunderstanding with slightest provocation, they send innocent people's lives into dust on insignificant and petty matters. They get ultimate pleasure for such acts. They create a farce by painting the color of adultery on innocent and pious souls. Aha? Simpleton!

Shyamali- sister of a person like Shyamalendu- the man denouncing Devbandya as an adulteress for the first time; has burnt many a like Bikram in the fire of her beauty and yet are seen as pure!

And Sharada Prasanna- accusing Amitav as characterless had evicted him from his house- his history is also not unknown to Amitav. And Sister Tuni---- shit! It is better not to think about them.

It is so late in the night. Amitav was not able to catch up sleep. Pushing all other notion aside, thoughts of that simple, innocent Devbandya circled back to his mind. Amitav being unable to find out a way to save her from this misfortune was in frequent despair.

'Amitav, Amitav'- hearing a female voice outside the home with a shock, he opened the door.

'You! Devi?' He was astonished to see Devi.

Without uttering anything, Devbandya entered inside. Her face appeared pale and she was trembling terribly.

Amitav moved closer to her and asked, "How come! You came so late in the night? Who else is with you?'

Devbandya said- nobody else, I am alone

-You are so late to my home?

- It is better to die in the heaven of your home than living in that hell with so much of suffering.

Amitav was not able to comprehend anything. Is he not seeing a dream?

No- he is not asleep! Being awake, can someone see a dream?

Amitav was thinking this night is unlike those accidental two nights of the yesterdays!

The first night was of ages. Shyamalendu visited him with a request to marry Shyamali so late in that night. He had refused point blank then. Insulted, Shyamalendu had left threatening him to take revenge of this insult.

Then the second night- when Bikram had visited!. After marrying Shyamali and being excessively drunk, had returned back rambling a lot to express his mental condition.

And tonight! His own Devi has reached home alone in the solitary night. Dumbfounded for few seconds and looking at Devbandya, he said-'Devi, It is not advisable for you to come to my home so late in the night.'

Devbandya lost all limits of her patience. All accumulated pain and suffering of previous days together tried to come out with a ripple effect. Without uttering a word, she started crying.

Amitav had never imagined in life that he is going to face a situation like this. He couldn't resolve what to do. He stood still.

After a while Devbandya said, "I have left home forever. There is no hope or trust on me in this world. Do you realize what will be my condition if you remove me from home without giving me a shelter?"

-But what will people talk about if you stay with me?

Devbandya smiled- some kind of a sadistic smile. She said, "You are such a coward! So much fearful you are about the society? I had strong conviction that you are a rebel, a progressive person. It is not nice on your part to be fearful about what people will say."

Amitav remained silent.

Devbandya again asked- Still you are silent, Amitav?

Amitav was answerless.

"You must be thinking that being a free willed woman, I have left home. But it is not true. What a person will do when she crosses the limit of patience. You don't know Amitav, in between torture of each family member increased so high that it became unbearable for me to stay put at home. Then I decided that before dying there, at least I should meet you once."

In a grave voice, Amitav said, "You sleep on the bed in this room. I will sleep outside. It's so late in the night."

Devbandya followed Amitav's words like an obedient child.

15

Next day it was chaos at Sharada Prasanna's residence. Devbandya was not seen at home. Sharada Prasanna lost his mind. How much of disrepute this news will bring to his status once people come to know about this news that Sharada Prasanna's daughter has eloped from home. There is no choice than crying at home like a thief's mother.

Pacifying Sharada Prasanna, Abhay, the elder son in law said, "It is good that the adulterous girl has left home or else nobody can estimate how much of bad omen she can bring in future".

Sharada Prasanna is not a person to break down like this. He remained patient.

Whatever has happened has already happened. What will be the result of crying further?

Wife said- "She must have gone to Amitav- bring her back".

By hearing this statement of wife, Sharada Prasanna irritatingly said, "No, that's not possible. Who so ever has left this home without my knowledge; the doors are always shut for them. She no more has a place in this house."

With this few words, the wife remained silent.

Devbandya is a slander on the family. She is past. She is an offender. She has blessed the family by voluntarily moving on her own.

Sharada Prasanna's thoughts were going haywire. He was experiencing hot, nasal breathing, He started thinking of ways to take revenge. He was getting impatient to punish a characterless person like Amitav for whom his family has to face such a misery.

Whatever Sharada Prasanna says- he does it- there are many previous instances of the same. He had no doubt about the fact that he can create havoc in Amitav's life.

16

Father had come! Amitav's father: along with Anita- his sister.

Surprised by seeing Devbandya inside the house, grudgingly father asked, "Who is this girl Amitav?"

-She is a poor helpless soul.

Before Amitav could utter anything, father howled "So you have opened an orphanage here. I had so much faith on you. I could never imagine even in my dream that you will stoop down to such low levels. All those gossips in the village about you are certainly turning true."

Perplexed, Amitav said- "You are misreading me father. Devi is also your daughter. You shouldn't misunderstand any of us."

Unrelentingly father went on- "I had so many dreams about you. Anita just finished her matric examination. She has also got a seat in the college here. I had decided to make her stay here with you and study."

Anita said- "Father! Sister Devi and I -both can stay together. Brother is always busy working outside. I will not feel lonely."

Listening to what Anita said, father got further agitated and said- "You shut up Anita. I will not permit you to live with a characterless girl who can stay alone with a man! Amitav- if you can remove the girl from this house- all problems can be resolved in one go."

But I am not capable to do so- father. Amitav said in a polite yet resolute voice.

Father stood up – he was trembling in anger – "I am telling you for the last time Amitav. Unless you remove that girl from this house, you will cease to have any relationship with me."

Amitav's head started reeling. What will he do? He is facing an intense problem like Bishu Moharana. What an answer he will give? His father is very stubborn.

Whatever he says, he hardly takes them back.

Father, mother, younger brother, sister and Devi- what will he do? Will he ask Devi to leave the house? But who is with her? Who will give her a shelter? So he will not keep any relationship with family! Family life may run smoothly if he doesn't keep any relationship with them. But if he asks Devi to leave, it will be a disaster for her. No it will never happen. Come whatsoever may be- he can't remove her from his home.

Father again repeated the same question- what answer is Amitav left with to give him!

Amitav opened his mouth- "Father, please doesn't

misunderstand me or Devi. Is Devi not your daughter? Please tell me what the poor girl will do if we remove her from home?"

Father almost roared back this time. He said- "Ok, why don't you talk straight and tell that you don't wish to keep any relationship with us?"

-What are you saying father? In a broken voice, Amitav could speak this much only.

-I am telling you the truth. From today assume that you have no one in your life—and I will also accept that my eldest son Amitav is dead for me.

Saying this much, along with Anita, father paced out of the room. Amitav couldn't stop him. He was standing like a frozen statue.

Devbandya could hear everything from outside. Moving closer to Amitav, she said in a sobbing voice- "What did you do Amitav?"

-Whatever I have done is correct. I don't want your advice on this matter.

-But for me you left your father, mother, brother and sister!!

- Don't hurt me Devi. Whatever I have done is right.

-Please go home and bring back your father. I will leave this place.

- That is impossible. I will never make that happen. I know-whatever storm may come, if we are pure and pious nothing wrong will happen to us.

17

Amitav had moved out of home on some emergency work.

Devbandya was there alone in that peculiar room of Amitav. Everything seemed odd here in this room. Those wonderful toys, heaps of books; old letters and photo albums scattered inside the room! He doesn't have an ounce of faith on God. But Gita, Bible, Quran and Tripitaka were lying on the table- how strange this site is? She has never seen such an improbable person before.

Returning home late in every night, he plays with that bald, dwarf joker with an enlarged tommy and then starts writing. Devbandya couldn't comprehend what time he actually sleeps. Up from the bed early in the morning, she finds him busy in reading and writing.

Amitav is strange! Who is Devi for him? Nobody- but he has estranged his relationship with father, mother and other siblings for her only.

No- he didn't distance himself. They have moved on their own.

Devbandya thought herself to be a bad omen. Wherever she went, she created a holocaust. Yes she couldn't identify her mistakes.

Whose mistake is this? Is it Amitav's? No-No- that is impossible- that cannot be!

Amitav will lever commit a mistake like this- but whose mistake is this for which they are suffering. Mistake is that of the society; the deformed blue glass needs to be removed from one's eyes. But is it that easy?

Not at all
To achieve this- you need a revolution, a war –like the last mass-revolution in Russia. Suppressed and oppressed, the rulers and the ruled, all of them have to merge. Then only no one has to ever face the misery.

Is it possible?

Is it possible in India and particularly in Odisha... a mass revolution—where democracy has no meaning? Here democracy has one meaning- that derives power from cooperative monarchy. A monarch tortured before and now they are doing the same as a group.

A revolution is possible against a single monarch but it is impossible to fight against many oppressors.

We are all dead. Paying taxes after taxes, we are unable to open our mouth and continue to live in poverty.

The chastity of mothers and sisters are robbed off in front

of our eyes but we enjoy these images as a bystander only. Are we human anymore?

No- we are just corpses in the name of humane.

It has become our hubby to step back than step forward. It has become our religion to go beneath the earth than climbing up in the ladder.

If someone climbs up, we will drag down the person. This is the misfortune of the nation.

Is there no end to this misery? No end to this oppression?

Devbandya's mind turned rebellious. Mass awakening is needed for this change. Amitav's magazine will be capable of evoking self-rights amongst common man.

Erroneous thinking has become a virtual borne habit of common man. Will they misunderstand Amitav or his efforts?

Whatever may happen, it is essential to awaken the society by removing the blindfold?

To achieve this, she will put whatever impossible effort is required and assist Amitav on his goals.

Fifteenth August is only seven days away. Amitav's magazine will be published on that day. Amitav has ascertained that his magazine is not going to be the mouth piece of petty minded politics: It will be a forceful vehicle to awaken and strengthen society, culture and literature.

Amitav's devotion ought to succeed; with folded hands, Devbandya prayed to the God. She has prayed many a times for an atheist like Amitav. Amitav will laugh aloud if he hears all this and say -If God can do everything then our society must not have been suffering like this! Was it possible to have such type of hypocrisy in our society in the name of the poor God!

So as per Amitav's opinion the word God is like a purchasing material. Selfish people are using this word in multifarious ways for their own benefits.

Amitav's words are not lies. Devbandya knows the entire misdeed done on the premise of God. Despite all this, for long years she has enough weakness for God from the deepest corner of her heart. She had an assumption that God is like another form of Amitav- calm, silent, simple and wide hearted. So she prays every day to him. It is true that Amitav is an atheist. But he has never asked her once to restrain from this activity. He is really strange… very strange.

Devbandya thought about how many days she would run a life with so much of uncertainty. As if there is no place for her in this world. Now onwards her life will be spent on this turbulent combustion.

Leaving home, she had come to Amitav. She had assumed that she would live with an assurance. But all her dreams are shattered now. People have started gossiping by demeaning her relationship with Amitav. That's the reason why Amitav is staying serious for last few days. Amitav is getting inglorious for her shake only.

Devbandya couldn't think further. She slept silently.

18

The fire of revenge intensified in Sharada Prasanna's heart. He will take revenge. He will take revenge against that ugly, characterless Amitav. He will wipe out the name of this person from this earth who has spoiled his prestige and self-esteem.

Or else he will continue to burn in the fire of evil throughout his life. Shyamalendu had spoken that Amitav's new magazine will be released on Fifteenth of August. Anxiously Sharada Prasanna glanced through the calendar. Today is Twelfth of August. In between only two days are left. Once Amitav's magazine is published, he will be immortal for his efforts and devotion. So he has to find a way out before that.

Will this meager issue be impossibility for Sharada Prasanna? No, that's not true. Sharada Prasanna will surely keep his words. He has done business of wagon loads of sugar and cement without a valid permit; will it be difficult for a person who has drawn lakhs of rupees against false bills from government without supplying goods to teach a lesson to a person like Amitav? No, it's very easy. In a few moments, he can wipe out the name of Amitav from this earth. For this he doesn't have to depend on someone's help or empathy or compassion.

Sharada Prasanna was extremely agitated. Pulling out the revolver from the drawer, he tested and loaded the bullets. This one will punish Amitav. He will shoot him to death. He could have done this small work by someone else but there will be a special pleasure in giving him punishment on his own hand.

19

Today is August 14th.

Tomorrow is a memorable day for India. This day will be a day to cherish for years to come for both Amitav and Devbandya.

It's almost eleven in the night. Amitav is yet to return. Beneath Amitav's bed, Devbandya glanced through the torn posters which she could discover minutes before.

Oh! What rubbish language is used to write about them? What kind of an ugly campaign was running in between by linking Devbandya with Amitav?

Tearing the posters from the walls somewhere, Amitav had hidden them here! He had never spoken a word to her. Does he not love Devi like before?

No, that can never happen! Rather he is in deep love with her. Deliberately he has kept these things away from her as she may be deeply hurt by knowing about all these crap.

Devbandya couldn't decide her course of action. Knowingly or unknowingly, she doesn't want to trouble Amitav. He is not a human being.. He is God and she doesn't want to put any blur on an august and godly person like Amitav. All these problems will automatically solve if she leaves this place. As such all the problems at family front got solved after she left her home.

Few days before Amitav had asked her- "Will you honor a request of mine, Devi?"

Devbandya was surprised! What's that Amitav is going to request her? She consented. She said, "You have sacrificed a lot for me. I will surely keep my word."

"Will you get married?" Amitav asked with a smile.

-Marry? Whom? Devbandya asked with a surprise.

Amitav said with a smile, "I will arrange a very good boy for you."

"Who is going to marry characterless and adulterous girl like me? You shouldn't waste your time prodding over matters like this. There is no need in my life to be married."

-But you have promised to keep my request!

-I will be delighted if I can make you happy. I am ready to accept your request- or order –for that anything- not only once- but you have the right to ask me throughout my life.

Amitav appeared sufficiently emotional on that day!

Devbandya was wondering what to do in the current situation. It is already half past twelve in the night. Amitav is yet to return. It will not be nice to go back before his return- should she travel back secretly like a thief?

What else she can do? She is always helpless to utter a word in front of Amitav and even though she can say all this- Amitav will be able to restrain her from leaving at that time of the night. But where will she go? Who will give her a shelter? Should she kill herself?

No, that's not possible, she won't attempt a suicide. Hearing this Amitav will hate whole of his life even after her death. But where will she go?

Yes, she will return to that powerful business tycoon Sharada Prasanna. Thereafter no pamphlet will be pasted on Amitav's walls and he can be relieved from the emerging unbearable pain.

Then she wrote a small letter and kept it on the table before leaving his home.

20

Returning around half past one in the night, Amitav was surprised to not find Devbandya at home. He couldn't comprehend first. Suddenly his eyes reached a letter on the table. He picked it up and started reading- Devbandya had written to Amitav.

Amitav
You are God for me. Being with you here, I don't want to spoil your reputation. I am an adulterous girl. Wherever I go, I invite evil. You may live at peace once I move out from here. No abusive posters will be pasted on walls by adding both of our names. You have sacrificed enough for me. I will remain indebted throughout my life.

Devi.
Everything around Amitav started revolving. What did Devi do? Will she not attempt suicide? Amitav was disturbed. In search for Devi, he started running like a mad man in the sleeping highway. At possible cost, he has to bring back Devi.

21

Armed with a loaded pistol, with utmost carefulness, Sharada Prasanna alighted from his jeep near Amitav's house and found the main door open. Neither Amitav nor Devbandya were there. Seeing this, he got doubly angry.

Whatever it may be, he has to take revenge today only.

Knowing well that he is looking for both of them, Amitav along with Devi must be hiding somewhere outside the home. They will surely return back after the fearful night ends. So he parked the jeep at a safe distance on the road side and sat on the corner of the house with the loaded pistol. As soon as Amitav arrives, the first bullet will pierce through his chest.

It was half past four in the morning; still Amitav had not returned. By that time Sharada Prasanna had lost his patience. He was enflamed on the fire of revenge. Without finding any other option, he gathered all the books of Amitav on his bed and emblazon them using kerosene. Watching the rising flames emanating from the fire, with a gratifying laugh he started his jeep.

It was almost morning then. After covering some distance,

he could see a small crowd on the road. He stopped the jeep and inquired about the incidence. Somebody responded with the information about a truck crushing a person in the night.

Inquisitively, he alighted from the jeep to reach the accident site and saw Amitav's body lying in the pool of blood on the road.

Sharada Prasanna stood like a frozen element. His eyes were filled with tears. This was not sympathetic tears towards Amitav; these were tears of a defeat- that he couldn't take revenge on Amitav before his death. With closed eyes, he stood still for few more moments.

He opened his eyes to find people loading Amitav's body with flower garlands. Everyone was giving a farewell to him with tearful eyes.

Far from a distance on someone's radio the national anthem could fill the air ... jana gana mana..... adhinayak jayahe ....

Sharada Prasanna rushed back to his jeep and ignited the engine again....

BLACK EAGLE BOOKS

www.blackeaglebooks.org
info@blackeaglebooks.org

Black Eagle Books, an independent publisher, was founded as
a nonprofit organization in April, 2019. It is our mission to
connect and engage the Indian diaspora and the world at large
with the best of works of world literature published on a
collaborative platform, with special emphasis on
foregrounding Contemporary Classics and New Writing.